George William Lloyd

The Devil in Dixie

George William Lloyd

The Devil in Dixie

ISBN/EAN: 9783337343392

Printed in Europe, USA, Canada, Australia, Japan

Cover: Foto ©Andreas Hilbeck / pixelio.de

More available books at **www.hansebooks.com**

The Devil in Dixie:

A Tale of the Times.

SERIO-COMICAL, SEMI-HISTORICAL, AND QUASI-DIABOLICAL.

" SATIRE'S my weapon.   .   .   .

.   .   .   .   .   .

O sacred weapon! left for Truth's defence!

.   .   .   .   .   .

Truth guards the poet, sanctifies the line,
And makes immortal, verse as weak as mine."—POPE.

" LIBERTY ! Freedom ! Tyranny is dead !
Run hence, proclaim, cry it about the streets ;
Some to the common pulpits, and cry out:
Liberty, freedom, and enfranchisement !"—SHAKESPEARE.

NEW-YORK:
AMERICAN NEWS COMPANY,
121 NASSAU STREET.
1865.

INTRODUCTORY.

In homespun language, and in jingling verse,
It is the poet's purpose to rehearse
Some things which have been chronicled, and some
Concerning which, as yet, the historian's mum.
And whether he'll succeed, or whether stick,
He scouts the shallow, worn, pedantic trick
Of going on marrow-bones to "invoke the muses."
No heathen he, nor fop.   He rather chooses
To hold *himself* to answer for his style,
Whether the critic favor or revile.
If praise be merited, no praise he'll lack ;
If blame, he'll bear it on his own broad back.

THE DEVIL IN DIXIE.

PART I.

TIME, A.D. 1782–3.

MANY years ago, as old chronicles show,
(Where discovered, I stay not to tell you now)
An alarming stir shook the regions below ;
And Satan, with all his imps, great and small,
Floundered strangely about in the fiery glow,
Stirring up an incandescent squall.
Oh ! dread wás the sight ; enough to affright
And set all a-quaking a weak mortal wight,
To witness the rushing, stampeding, and crushing,
The stumbling, sprawling, elbowing, and pushing,
That madly ruled in that world of night.
For seven long days, from various ways,
Came fiends a-trooping and all a-blaze ;
It seemed as if hell had turned out, pell-mell,
Its remotest squatter, on purpose to swell
Those crowds so filled with alarm and amaze.

On, on they came in squadrons of flame;
Spirits of noble and ignoble name;
The tall and the stately, the squat and the lame;
The devils that do the dirty work,
And the aristocratic that mean labor shirk,
And ride over the rest in their race for fame.
(I must tell you this in parenthesis,
Not deeming it wise such a chance to miss—
That down in those regions of drought and dearth,
In that world of shades, there are numerous grades
Of society, just like we have on earth;
And the " top-sawyer" there his rank parades.
Nay, we copied, I know, from those gentry below,
Our many distinctions of wealth, race, and birth.)

But what was this rumpus and uproar about?
You are ready to ask me, without a doubt;
Why such a commotion? Wait, sirs, I've a no-
    tion,
That by dint of a proper amount of devotion
On the part of the poet, 'twill all come out.
For we mean to constrain this fiendish train,
In rhythmical measure and musical strain,
To tell the truth; yes, the devil, forsooth,
Though he squirm with reluctance, and crave our
    ruth,
Shall tell a true story, at least in the main.

Well, then, to account for this uproar in hell—
For I'll come to it straight; not stopping to dwell
On collateral or introductory matter,
Nor wishing your sensitive nerves to shatter,
The wonderful story I'll haste to detail.

When the last imp had come 'neath the fiery
    dome
That arches over the desolate home
Of the father of evil, best known as " the Devil,"
The scene of many a "scrimmage" and revel,
And the tumult had somewhat subsided, behold!
A marvellous sight succeeded the scrabble;
There uprose a tall throne, that like burnished
    gold
Reflected the flames that surged round the rabble.
Then forward there came, towering high o'er the
    flame,
The arch-fiend, Diabolus—mark you, the same
That eluded so deftly the vigilant warden
Of Adam and Eve in the primitive garden,
And cunningly duped our ancestral dame.
Ah! 'tis no mistake; that form was old Satan's,
With caudal appendage, the greatest of great 'uns
That flapped on hell's billows, and lashed the foam
    higher,
Or trailed in repose on its flooring of fire.

The traditional horns and cloven hoof
Were, besides, incontrovertible proof
That he was the potent chief and commander
Of those crowds of the genus Salamander.
    Well, the Fiend stalked on, and ascended the
            throne ;
His eyes gleamed like fire with malice and ire,
As he seated him there all high and alone ;
His nostrils and mouth vented streams of flame,
While around him his myrmidons trooping came ;
'Twas a sight to behold 'most bewildering and dire.
Then the trumpets of hell, with discordant yell,
Sounded a flourish, and silence fell
On the unclean host ; and, with upturned look,
They waited until Diabolus spoke,
And what he said, if you'll listen I'll tell.

" Fellow-devils," said he, " it is plain to see,
Our schemes are foiled up in yonder world ;
Freedom's flag is victorious, so lately unfurled ;
Our good friend King George's Red-coats are hurled
Back o'er the Atlantic, sore routed ; ah, me !
It was my fond hope to have seen a stout rope
Round the neck of that man that's made monarchy
            ' slope ;'
My snares, spun and woven so subtle and fine,
I had warily laid with this very design,

That he and compatriots should dance to the tune
Of 'God save the King,' in the air, pretty soon;
But, lo! they all straddle triumphant in saddle,
And King George's men are all on the skedaddle!
   I need not now mention how great the attention
I've paid to the 'Land of the Pilgrims' for ages;
It has been to me matter of constant reflection,
In what way I could foil those old Puritan sages;—
Holding on with my well-known powers of reten-
      tion,
I established a special Bureau of Inspection,
Whose business it was to make a collection
Of figures and facts for my guidance, how best
I could break up that very annoying nest
Of men who love Liberty, civil and sacred.
Then, I scattered among them Discord and Hatred,
And burst them asunder in various sects;
Threw plenty of bones of contention and strife
Among them, to alienate and to vex,
And set them to worry each other for life.
I set by the ears Independent and Quaker;
At loggerheads put Presbyterian and Shaker—
No, stop! I forgot; there were no Shakers then;
Presbyterian and Baptist is what I mean.
   Then, by way of a change, I tried to derange
Those hard-headed fellows, by causing a strange

Wild feeling to seize them 'bout wizards and
    witches,
Till their nerves were unstrung or jerking with
    twitches.
I made them believe, while I laughed in my
    sleeve,
That the country was full of hags, young and old,
Who body and soul to myself had sold,
On no other terms, than, in consideration,
They may have the agreeable gratification
To cause whom they pleased to pine, sicken, or
    grieve;
To inflict on their foes a good scarification;
And torture them sorely with pains of damnation.
Thus I got them engaged in a holy rage,
Such as hadn't been known for many an age;
'Twas all they could think of, both learned and rude,
In the crowded mart and the wild-solitude,
To hunt up the heretic sinners and witches;
Imprison the former, and, spite of their screeches,
The latter hang up for the general good.
    These plans for a time seemed to work most sub-
    lime;
And Liberty howled lest her empire was gone;
And Religion gave vent to a terrible groan;
There was nothing but seemed with my wishes to
    chime.

But at length Common Sense, long held in sus-
    pense,
Shook her locks of strength, and asserted her
    right
To the throne of the mind, and suppressed the af-
    fright
My spell over sinner and saint had cast ;
So my hope of gaining by this was past,
Notwithstanding I spared neither pains nor ex-
    pense.
    What next to do, was the question to view ;
You'd better believe 'twas a puzzler, too !
And my mind for a time was greatly perplexed ;
Till at last I discovered ' John Bull ' was vexed
With the saucy talk of the men of the West.
John, seeming determined his power to test,
Had jerked up the reins of government tighter,
While Jonathan ' guessed' that they should have
    borne lighter.
Thinks I to myself, I shall gain from this clatter
A pretty good lift, or I'll know what's the matter.
I thought I could put the thing through to my
    mind,
By stirring up John to go it blind !
So I went to work with the zeal of a Turk,
'Neath St. James' Cabinet table did lurk ;
And among the results of my smartness and wit,

I got John to levy a tax upon tea,
Well knowing the Yankees would squirm, d'ye see,
And show their grit without pausing a bit;
Then John, who was strong as a bull could be,
Would rush to the fray, deal hit for hit,
And smash up the temple of Liberty.
    Then what a commotion on land and on ocean
Followed close upon this, you very well know;
For you all lent a hand, like good devils, I trow.
You mind how we grinned at that smart Yankee
      notion,
Getting up the 'Tea-Party' in Boston, to go
And dump a whole ship-load of tea in the water;
Ah! ha! my dear devils, I cried, we have caught
      her!
I couldn't have helped things along in a shorter
Or handier manner than this—that's so!
Now, then, for the tug, said I with a shrug
Of delight, I have got things fixed quite snug;
The hare-brained fellows around those diggings
Seem determined to follow up what they've begun;
And when King George's men, with sword, mus-
      ket, and gun,
Came in ships of all sizes, and all kinds of rig-
      gings,
I shrewdly suspected we'd see some fun;
For them Yankee chaps don't know how to run.

So I hoped they would get particular fits,
And the shrine of Freedom be battered to bits.
   But I need not detail, for the news would be
      stale ;
And your memories supply each fact without fail,
Of the various movements on flood and field,
And of how John Bull has been forced to yield.
Ah, me ! my imps, it gives me the gripes
To see that bunting of ' Stars and Stripes '
So saucily flinging its folds to the breeze,
And claiming respect on land and seas.
It's an ugly look for my cause, I ween,
And the darkest day I ever have seen !
The hopes of the human race will rise,
With that flag a-floating before their eyes ;
Despots and aristocrats will quail,
And bigoted ecclesiastics grow pale ;   [out,
For they'll deem that their games are all played
Now King George's men have faced right about,
And his rabble of Hessians are put to the rout."
   And here the emotions of poor Old Nick
Overmastered him quite, and his voice grew thick ;
And great red-hot tears, like molten steel,
Down his storm-scarred visage did rapidly steal ;
And the old lion-hearted Beelzebub
Was compelled with all his might to blub-
Ber, until Pandemonium did shake and reel.

A sight so pathetic as that might well
Have moved the most hard-hearted imps in hell.
And it did move them, too; for they all howled
      sore
With anguish, until they could howl no more;
While a score of the strongest, than pine-trees
      taller,
And muscles like oaks of a thousand years,
Supported their chief, for fear he would fall, or
The fiery roof shake about their ears.

    But grief spent its strength, and a calm at length
Came over these troubled spirits once more;
Though Diabolus scarcely voided a tenth
Of the fire and sulphur he'd voided before;
And it took him some time—I must say in my
      rhyme—
To recover his pulse, which had fallen much lower
Than was ever the case in any past time;
And his poor old heart still continued sore.

    He resumed his remarks, but in tremulous tones,
And interrupted with sighs and groans,
That still found vent from the gullets of those
Whose emotions had risen to higher levels
Than had been attained by colder devils;
And therefore took all the more time to subside,
And placidly flow with the common tide;
At least that's the reason, as I suppose.

"My fiends," said he, "it appears to me,
(It was all he could do to get the words out,)
We're in a perplexing fix, without doubt,
And, our interests being in jeopardy,
Your collective wisdom is urgently needed,
As to how we can best repair this rout,
That our darling project be no more impeded,
Nor the cause of Human Freedom succeeded
By another such lucky and prosperous bout
As those Western fellows have just perfected.
Nay, it is most true, we are bound to undo
The doings of Mister Washington ;
And if the business be longer neglected,
We shall surely our culpable laziness rue,
And be forced to acknowledge *ourselves* undone.
Now, my devils true, say, what shall we do
To remedy this unexpected defeat ?
I want your advice in less than a trice ;
Let each wise imp state his particular view
Of the matter in hand, and I'll make my choice—
I'm determined—before I leave this seat."

Now I cannot begin to describe the din
That rose on the thick sulphureous air,
And through those cavernous regions resounded ;
'Twas "confusion" *ten thousand times* "worse
    confounded ;"

'Twas Bedlam transferred to those realms of sin;
And sufficient the stoutest heart to scare.

   Diabolus saw they were wasting time;
So, raising his full-length form sublime,
He struck three times his enormous tail
On the back of his throne with force tremendous;
'Twas a signal he never had known to fail
In quieting even the most stupendous
Excitement among his unruly crew;
And it answered on this occasion, too.   .

   So the rabble vast was in silence hushed;
Then in regular form the confab began;
And onward the stream of eloquence ran,
Or rather, like Niagara, rushed,
As each one his favorite plan proposed,
And the why and the wherefore at length dis-
     closed.
But to tell all the measures that were propounded,
How the deepest depths of cunning were sounded,
Would far exceed my descriptive powers,
And task your patience for hours and hours;
Besides, I'd be cramming your aching head
At a time when you ought to be snoozing a-bed.
But the final decision I'll try to unfold,
As the tale *in extenso* can't now be told.

   The most sapient devil among the crew,
And one who had had a great deal to do

With earthly matters, put forth the opinion
That over the rest was allowed the dominion.
I will give, in his language, as near as I can,
The substance of this, the accepted plan :

" Most mighty Diabolus! listen," said he,
" And worthy imps, all attend unto me;
For I think I a feasible plan can see;
I have had it some time under consideration;
And I'll lay it before you, without hesitation.
    You must know, though the mortals up yonder
        have crossed
Many schemes and designs upon which we have
        doted,
Yet our cause is a long way from being lost;
Our industry hasn't been all in vain,   .
Nay, on the whole, a decided gain.
How oft our delighted eyes have gloated
O'er the mental anguish and bodily pain
Men at times have inflicted, at times have en-
        dured !   .
Why, my fellow-imps, you may be assured,
I have often felt jealous and angry to see
How they rival us devils in cruelty !
And then, they are selfish as selfish can be,
Despotic, licentious, proud, and malignant;
I vow, I can hardly help feeling indignant;

For us, their instructors, they almost exceed':
We must study hard, fellow-devils, indeed,
Or I shan't be surprised if they yet take the lead!
　Now every fiend of common-sense
Cannot fail to see, as a consequence,
Our capital yet is of vast amount,
And all standing ready to turn to account.
Nay, up to the time of my hastening here,
I have kept it pretty well floating there,
'Mong the very folks.whose especial affairs
Are the subject now of our onerous cares.
Don't you know that for years, my worthy com-
　　　peers,
We have had a most flourishing school of instruc-
　　　tion
In both Eastern and Western Hemispheres ?—
And how this thing, *so weighty,* your minds failed
　　　to cross,
I declare, to account for, I'm quite at a loss !—
The system is one of *our own* construction,
And wisely designed for the thorough reduction
Of civilized man to a savage state ;
To foster cupidity, cruelty, hate ;
To obfuscate the reason, and harden the heart;
And, indeed, fit the pupil to act well the part
Of a very respectable devil.　And so,
To illustrate what foresight we fiends possess,

It is only just needful for me to show
An historical fact.   'Tis no more nor less
Than this:—Ah ! I see you're beginning to guess !
You're intelligent devils, I must confess.
I'll proceed, though, in spite of your manifest wit;
For I still can enlighten your noddles a bit,
My experience having been wide and plenty:
　In the year one thousand six hundred and
　　　　twenty—
The very same year that the ' Pilgrims ' landed
On Plymouth Rock—we'd contrived, you know,
That a matter of twenty negroes, or so,
Should be in the ' Old Dominion ' stranded.
The ship's captain sold them all in a trice ;
And we took good care it should be at a price
To make it worth while as a speculation :
And, maugre all fear of coming damnation,
For pirates of Britain, and Holland, and Spain,
And Portugal, also, to voyage the main
For plethoric cargoes of African savages.
Nor was it a matter of serious objection,
Or cause of unpleasant, foreboding reflection,
That Africa's wild and uncivilized plains .
Should witness such horrible, pitiless ravages,
As the lust of these devils incarnate incited.
Ah ! don't you remember how we were delighted
At this most successful result of our pains ?

And how, when the merciless villains displayed
Such perfect delight in the murderous trade,
We thought we might safely leave all its affairs
In their blood-spattered hands, while our arduous
    cares
Were devoted to matters more needing our aid?
  Well, just look how the business has grown on
      their hands,
And covered with slaves yonder Western lands!
A thousand ships' decks are red with the stains
Of the negro's blood; and the clanking of chains
Is heard far and wide, from Ontario's wave,
To where Mexico's Gulf doth the Continent lave!
Only here and there is a free spot left,
That has not witnessed the devilish theft
Of man from himself!   Yes, those *Liberty-lovers*
Are steeped to their chins in the blood of the
    slave;
Are the cronies of vile pirātical rovers,
That trade in the bodies and souls of men!
  Now, these facts are exceedingly cheering; but
      then,
There's another side to the question, I trow;
There are many amongst them, I'd have you know,
Who are made up of stern old Puritan stuff;
And who deem they have had rather more than
    enough

Of the blood and the sweat, the shrieks and the
    tears
Of the wretched bondman; and they talk right
    along
About 'violence,' 'cruelty,' 'outrage,' and 'wrong;'
Expressing, with constant remonstrance, their fears
That the vengeance of Heaven will not tarry long,
Ere it smite with destruction and ruin profound
The nation thus trampling the poor in the ground.
Nor are they content with talking, alone;
I'm, moreover, aware that Heaven's high throne
Is besieged by these men with vehement cries,
That the Just and Holy One would arise
To deliver those whom the tyrants despise
And trample upon. And besides, the prayers
Of the victims themselves ascend with theirs;
And too well we know the disposition
Of Him we hate: though he may delay
For a while to make strict inquisition,
Yet may he, at no very distant day,
Arise in his strength, like an arméd man,
And crush with his irreversible ban
The whole of our dear man-stealing crew.
    But I'm looking a little too far ahead;
Let's confine our thoughts to the present instead.
    Now what I propose to do, if we can,
Is, to *turn* this sympathetic tide,

That already has flowed too far and wide;
And persuade these Puritans to decide
That the black-hided man is simply a beast
Of burden, or something near it, at least;
Or, failing of this, I would make them believe,
That, consistent with strictest piety,
They may take the scheme as a providence kind,
And wisely and opportunely designed,
For a ready-constructed *Mission Society*,
Through which these savages, mentally blind,
Might receive much more than a *quid pro quo*,
In the form of instruction in Gospel truth;
And so, these Christians, without any ruth,
Might behold the slave-ships come and go;
Regard the slave-trader a sort of 'stool-pigeon'
For trapping the blacks in the net of religion!
Nay, more, with clear conscience invest their cash
In a 'nigger or two,' and even the lash
Ply over their carcases, merely to prove
To those unsophisticated blacks,
How consistent it may be with Christian love,
To exact their labor, so *honestly* (!) bought,
By benevolent whacks on their naked backs;
In return for which, they'd be *orally* taught
To hopefully look for salvation *above!*

From this, it will be but a gentle transition,
To regard as a part of their holy mission,

The setting up of the *Auction-Block*
In every city and town in the land,
From the western waters to eastern strand,
Upon which to expose for convenient sale,
Their well-sleeked herds of human stock!
　And oh! dear devils, I'm greatly in error—
Nay, I would be willing to wager my life,
If there wouldn't ensue a grand 'Reign of Ter-
　　ror'—
If the wild and hope-expiring wail
Of the plundered father and heart-broken mother,
The vain cries of parted husband and wife,
Of outraged sister, and manhood-crushed brother,
At scenes like this, will not soon prevail
The voice of protesting Freedom to smother;
And finally lay, prostrated in dust,
That long-sighed-for object of human trust.
　And then we can help this business along—
If we can't, I think it would be a pity—
At the present juncture, by mingling among
Those American sages, in Congress met　.
At this very time in that famous 'City
Of Brotherly Love.' You do not forget
That that dignified body are gathered there,
From each of the Thirteen Colonies sent,
To settle the matter of government;

To enact such fundamental laws,
As, in view of the good of the common cause,
They shall, in their wisdom, see fit to declare
To be needful to join in a federal band
The several States; thus united to stand
For mutual defence and preservation,
On the basis firm of one common nation.
They are pretty good men, as the world goes, I
     know;
But yet, if it's needful, I'm ready to show
That they are not beyond diabolic temptation.
Already, indeed, I find that dissension
(And credit this fact to our cunning invention)
Is dividing their counsels. Those Puritan chaps,
Foreseeing disunion and other mishaps
May, probably, grow from the knavery
Of the mad devotees of slavery,
Want to stop the nefarious traffic in souls;
But the slaveocrats' power the council controls;
And if Puritan piety will not submit,
They will muster their forces and threaten to split.
So you see, fellow-devils, there's work for us there,
To assist them in putting their matters all square!
    Our interest, at once we shall see, if we're wise,
Is to help them concoct a Compromise;
'Twill be better for us than their splitting asunder,

If such a contingency should fall out;
Though I think they know better what they're
    about.
Because, just as soon as the foreign war-thunder
Is heard again on those Western shores,
With the view of settling up old scores,
They'll again join hands for the common defence;
And this new necessity pressing them hard,
The slavists will listen to common-sense,
And their favorite 'Institution' discard.
The result will be, such an organization   [nation
As will make them, ere long, the most powerful
That ever the sun looked down upon;
And our chance of strangling Freedom is gone.
    We must get them, I say, then, a League to
        agree to,
One of whose recognized objects shall be, to
Secure as the right of the dominant class,
The holding for ever the dark-skinned race
As a toiling and fettered substructural mass,
To be held and regarded as merely chattel,
In the same category with horses and cattle;
To be branded, or tortured with paddle or lash,
At the owner's pleasure or view of the case;
Or be even commercially turned into cash.
Or should the said chattel be ever so rash
As to give his master 'leg-bail,' and dash

For coveted liberty, then, *sans demur*,
As oft as a case like this shall occur,
To be caught, and rendered by process brief,
As though he were an assassin or thief.
All which to be settled as firm as can be,
By the binding prescription of *lex terræ*.*

   And thus, you perceive, not a rood of soil
Shall be free to those victims of fetters and toil,
Through all the fair and wide extent
Of *Freedom's* share of the continent!
Mountain and valley, forest and plain,
The shore of river and inland main,
The dreary wilderness solitude,
And the region of civilized habitude,
Populous city and ruined mound,
Swamp, prairie, and dell, rocky cleft, and cave,
All alike shall be hunting-ground,
Where canine, and more brutish *human* hound,
Shall run down the liberty-courting slave,
Who, to grasp his prize, shall embrace his grave.
   Oh! what jolly, delighted devils we'll be,
When the pleasing results of our policy
Shall gladden our eyes! for, listen to me ;
The hundredth part has scarcely been told ;
'Twould take me days—yes, weeks to unfold

* The law of the land.

The moral confusion 'twill bring about ;
The negro's enslavement's a trifling part
Of the purpose most dear to my pitiless heart.
'Tis but little that this inflated lout—
This stuck-up 'white'—shall deny the right,
To the victim crushed by his meanness and might,
To own himself, or children, or wife ;
And doom him to wear out his bitter life
In the dreary task of bringing grist
To the mill of *Freedom's Monopolist.*
    I fully expect that 'twill not be long,
Ere this race, so selfish, vain, and strong,
Claiming, forsooth, the name ' Caucasian,'
Will have little left of a human heart.
The lessons learned in Slavery's school,
And the tasted sweets of despotic rule,
Will for ever seal up the springs of compassion ;
And transform it into the counterpart
Of our own infernal brotherhood.
O fellow imps ! wont that be good ?
Oh ! sure it will be fun worth running to see,
These redoubtable *champions of Liberty* (!)
Mocking the wrongs of a prostrate race ;
And avowing Negro Bondage the base
Of all that's worth calling Human Rights ;
And the brand, and the whip, and the coffle, and all
The devilish adjuncts of chattel-thrall,

Not only consistent, but needful even
To constitute the patriot's heaven;
That he the most of manliness shows,
Who at every ' nigger ' turns up his nose,
And has every vein in his bosom froze,
Preventing sympathy's tide to run
Toward the cheated, robbed, rogue-ridden one!
    More than this you'll espy, or tell me I lie;—
The tear of pity in *woman's* eye,
That men used to think became it so well,
Shall cease to sparkle with tremulous sheen;
Nay, her gentle heart shall cease to feel,
And become as hard as high-tempered steel;
And never again shall her bosom swell
In soft condolence with sorrow, I ween;
Enough for the stultified conscience shall be
The answer: ' Its only a nigger, you see!'
    Thus, my scheme will work a fine *social* muss.
Let me now its *political* side discuss.
But, no! I needn't on this long dwell;
In two or three words the results I'll foretell.
    If we can persuade them to make this arrange-
        ment,
In the hope of heading off future estrangement,
It will answer our purposes just to the nick,
By working in this satisfactory way,
The traders in human flesh will grow

More exacting and arrogant day by day ;
And the others will deem it politic
To let them bear unlimited sway
In the nation's affairs ; and will cringe and bow,
Not daring to say their souls are their own !
For fear of incurring the slaveocrat's frown,
Or worse—lest they'd tear the Union down.

    Thus, dear imps, we'll have a nice bone to pick
In a generation or two, at most ;
For that vaunted land of ' the noble free '
Will then be hectored by Slavery ;
And Freedom, pining with grief and shame,
At the meanness and villainy wrought in her name,
Her hopes all shattered, her purposes crossed,
Will lie down in despair, and give up the ghost ;
And Treason and Tyranny's banner shall wave
Victorious over her dishonored grave ;
And we, as happy as devils can be,
Will hold an infernal jubilee ;
And all the caverns and dungeons of Hell
Shall resound with the loud, triumphant yell
That announces the final success of our plan—
Blotting out the last hope of despairing man."

    The fiend ceased with this peroration ;
And it seemed as if the whole creation,
From its centre to its circumference,

Was shaken and heaved by the mighty shout
That arose from the throats of this impious rout.
They, one and all, applauded the sense,
The wit, the judgment, the eloquence
Of the specious imp who had raised their hope,
By indicating such marvellous scope
For the exercise, in a manner fit,
Of their infernal cunning and wit ;
And rapture gleamed from the fiery eyes
Of the grim and thunder-browed Prince of the Pit;
And he took his lieges all by surprise,
By descending from his lofty seat,
And rushing with open arms to greet
The imp who'd afforded them all such a treat.
  " My dear, my precious, my eloquent elf,
Thou very counterpart of myself !
I thank thee, as only Diabolus can,
For unfolding to us this exquisite plan.
I scarcely can tell which most to commend,
Thy head or thy heart ; and now I intend
To show my unqualified approbation
By advancing thee to the highest station
In this my Infernal Government.
Lo! honor and dignity, next to my throne,
I now vouchsafe as thy very own,
In the widest meaning and fullest intent."

The fiend bowed his caput low;
And, whether the rest were jealous or no,
They all applauded with one accord
The decree of their unrelenting lord.
They knew it would not avail to discuss
The right of precedence, or kick up a fuss;
For Lucifer's word was ever a law,
And for all their grumbling he'd care not a straw,
   His Satanic Highness proceeded to say,
That he wouldn't tarry another day;
But set out at once for the world above,
In order, without delay, to move
The powers he had at his command,
In setting a-going the business in hand.
And commanding his trusty guards to stand
All ready plumed, with himself to fly
With lightning wings to Dixie's land,
He adjourned the meeting *sine die*.
   So the rabble departed, as merry-hearted
As you could expect such a rabble to be;
At least, their eloquent brother 'd imparted,
To both devils of high and low degree,
A *modified* pleasure, to think that a chance
Was left them still their cause to advance,
And strike the death-blow of Liberty.
They were sanguine devils, every one;
And though Providence often spoiled their fun,

With each defeat their will grew the stronger,
And they held to their purpose the harder and
    longer,
Whenever they hoped a defeat to redress,
Or discovered a loophole that promised success.
    Forthwith, with eager and rapid pinions,
Diabolus flew with his trusty minions;
And the dismal realms of brooding night
And Stygian flood were soon lost to their sight;
And in far less time than it takes in my rhyme
To announce their flight, they did all alight
On the whirling orb upon which we dwell,
Though millions of leagues from the confines of
    Hell.
For to swim or to walk, to fly or to climb,
These devils could all do equally well,
And that in the briefest space of time.
No weariness felt they, nor staid they at all,
Till they landed in "Independence Hall;"
Some swooping down the chimney tall;
And others contracting their forms so small,
That the keyhole afforded them easy ingress
To the chamber where sat the American Congress.
Of course, they were all invisible
To the ken of the keenest mortal sight;
Indeed, they would have been baffled quite

In the object they sought, could they have been
     caught; ,
And all their designs would have come to naught,
And their schemes have turned out infeasible.
But being unseen by human eye,
Wherever they chose to creep or fly,
The wisest and best were exposed to the hap
Of falling into the devil's trap.
    And so it turned out in the present case;
Though the Devil didn't show his face,
You may traces find of his unclean paws,
If you take the trouble to look at a clause
Or two—nay, or *three*, of the Constitution
That closed up the work of the Revolution.
Thus, that famous American "*Magna Charta*,"
That the heroes of freedom wished, and that ought
     to
Have stood at the summit of human laws,
Was marred by the deep and ugly stain,
Of legally binding with stronger chain
An already fettered and prostrate race !
    Ah! then did Liberty hide her face
For very shame at her sons' disgrace;
And she trembled, lest her new-built fane
Should prove but a bubble, hollow and vain !
    But then this parchment celebrated,
And high 'mong legistical monuments rated—

By dint of consummate political wit,
'Twas contrived its forensic language should fit
The lofty views so ably stated
In that document known as " The Declaration
Of Independence," by which the nation
Had incontrovertibly vindicated
The right of every wronged aspirant
For liberty, to resist the tyrant;
And, claiming the boon the Creator gave,
Fight for it rather than be a slave.   [lieve it.
    So, 'twas couched in terms that men should be-
Never the chain of a *slave* would weld,
Nor forge a bolt, nor hammer a rivet;
But, "*persons to service or labor held*,"
Escaped, to their *claimants* should rendered be;
—Can't you the plain distinction see ?
'Tis as clear as the clearest mud to me !—
Then those *modest* claimants should have, moreover,
Through twenty yearly circles more,
The privilege granted them to recover
Other " persons " they *claimed* on *Africa's shore !*
You see, there's no issue that needs agitation
'Tween this and the Freeman's " Declaration !"
    O Devil ! most cunning, most shrewd, most wise !
Thine was a masterly compromise !
The blending of light with the darkness of night;
Of Slavery's wrong with Liberty's right;

The " iron and clay " of that image tall,
That of old, previsioned the rise and fall
Of Rome, whose sceptre ruled the world ;
Who at last, for her crimes, to perdition was hurled.
Well mightst thou expect that this impious fusion
Of good with evil, of truth with delusion,
Would one day lead to the wildest confusion
That jarring elements ever wrought ;
And, unless thy schemes be baffled, be fraught
With disaster and ruin, that needs must impart
Most boundless delight to thy ruthless heart !
But whether or no, foul anarchy's seeds
Are broadly sown throughout the nation ;
Concord like this to fell discord leads,
And prepares the land for such castigation
As devils, no doubt, would rejoice to see come,
But patriots pray to be rescued from !

But a truce to apostrophe ! let us proceed
To show the results of this sorry deed.

PART II.

AND now I'll presume you will just assume
That three fourths of a century, almost, elapse,
Since old Lucifer laid those wily traps,   .
In which he caught those short-sighted chaps
In that Philadelphia council-room,
Ere the scenes I am now about to unfold
Are in Pandemoniac annals enrolled.
The *place* is the same, though the *time* far apart;
That's all I need tell you, before I start,
On my story's second and final part.

I take you, then, once more to the den
Where the councils of devils, their feasts, fasts,
        and revels,
Are commonly held. Had I time, I would fain
Describe its appointments in graphic strain;
But I haven't. And yet you must stretch your
        travels

In thought, where I took you awhile ago,
In order the rest of my story to know.
  There's a rabble there now, and a mighty " tow-
     row ;"
But a *different animus* stamps their mien ;
The wrinkles of care are smoothed from the brow
Of every imp that graces that scene ;
All about them is joy, unmixed with alloy ;
Something's happened their former gloom to de-
     stroy ;
They have all heard encouraging news, I ween.
  Once more stalks Diabolus into that hall,
Where his lieges are mustered, great and small ;
And a pleasant smile lights his features grim—
A rather unusual look for him !
With his once faltering step now confident grown,
Again he ascends his flaming throne.
  Commanding silence by wave of hand,
His numerous hosts now facing him stand ;
He blandly greets them ; and, let me mention
Another act of his condescension :
He at once assumes a familiar air,
And calls them all "brothers !"—it made them
     stare.
They could scarcely realize where they were,
So much had Lucifer's sternness unbent,
And such kindness in every feature was blent.

" Brothers !" said he, " I have summoned you here,
To share in my rather uncommon cheer ;
To-day we shall join in a grand celebration,
That will make full amends for our past vexation.
Joy shall resound through my wide domains ;
Victory at last crowns our toils and pains ;
For we've fixed for certain yon Yankee nation.
For ages I've worked and watched for this day ;
It is come ! it is come, after long delay !
Prepare then, each one, for a high jubilation,
Such as never was known in my realms in the
          past,
And the memory of which shall for ever last.
    The programme is as follows : Attention, I
          pray !
First, let the artillery of Hell resound
An infernal salute of a thousand round ;
Let a million brazen trumpets bray ;   [fells
Let the gongs and the bells wake the gorges and
Of this fiery dominion that owns my sway :
And when the first gun has the racket begun,
Let every devil do his best,
In shouting, to show creation the zest
With which he hails the work so well done,
And the joy which Tophet's wide empire swells.
    And next, let a grand procession form—
You needn't mind, if the weather *is* warm ;

You can all stand heat, I know, pretty well;
We are all of us somewhat accustomed to dwell
In a climate that's *rather tropical !*
Well, then, the moment the signal blares,
Let the revellers all in order fall,   [squares,
And march through the principal streets, and
And roads, and avenues of this
My stately and royal metropolis.
Let my palace band, with its clamor grand,
In this mighty pageant lend a hand;
Let ten thousand flaunting banners stream,
Ten thousand volcanoes their fires gleam;
In short, neither cost nor labor spare,
Our rapturous, measureless joy to declare.
And lastly, let my subjects all
Assemble themselves in this regal hall,
To hear a synopsis of what has been done
In the land of Dixie to warrant this fun."

He said; and away the rabble all went
To carry this programme out intent;
And in less than a twinkle the cannon roared,
And the flaunting banners, by thousands, soared
From every tower and giddy height—
It was an exciting and wonderful sight;
But the favorite flag—you could count it by scores,
Was the *Devil's own flag—the " Stars and Bars !"*

Volcanoes sprang forth, by magic, it seemed,
And o'er the wild scene their fires gleamed;
The music rattled and crashed—you see,
We call it " music " *by courtesy.*
Such music !   No mortal, I do believe,
Could ever listen to it and live!

  The procession moved on in rollicking glee,
Surging along like a storm-lashed sea;
But the noise was greater than tempest e'er wrought,
Surpassing description, yes, even thought !
There were sights of wild wonder and novelty
To be seen wherever the vast mob went,
Grotesque in their nature, and grand in extent.
An air of triumph did all infect,
Each imp walking proudly with tail erect,
And many a one in that crowd could boast
On the tip of his tail a dead rebel's ghost !
One sported a Judge, who had made the decision,
That a black man in chains was his normal con-
        dition ;
On another's rode high a pro-slavery Preacher,
Who'd perverted the words of the heavenly Teach-
        er;
On another's was perched an Editor vile,
Who, to prop up his party, 'd told lies by the score ;
And secesh politicians, a thousand or more,
Decked the tails of as many imps in fine style ;

And they'd stuck ('tis as true as you ever were
    born)
A *pro-slavery Christian* on every horn!
  But, there! I must hold; for I cannot recite
A millionth part of this wonderful sight.
Suffice it, then, that I finally write—
There were diabolical fitness and taste
In the endless fixings that lavishly graced
This monster carnival of the Pit;
In short, 'twas a triumph of impish wit.
  The procession has ended its serpentine course,
And each devil has shouted until he is hoarse,
Yet still mad with joy as devil could be.
You may smile at the thought of felicity
Pervading the air of so dismal a den;
Yet 'tis true as the rest of my tale; but then,
Of course I am speaking *comparatively*.
It was, after all, such a *queer* sort of glee,
As I hope may ne'er visit you or me!
  And now they all stride through the portals
    wide,
That afforded them access on every side,
To the great council-chamber, where, sitting in
    state,
The grim old king did their presence await.
You wonder not how they all got in;
You knew before that these imps of sin

Can compress themselves into the smallest place,
Or expand, till they fill a tremendous space.
   But whose is that form on the orator's stand,
Thus smiling and bowing with gesture bland?
We have seen before that unique devil, sure!
Ah! yes, you remember the demagogue grand,
Who seventy years ago, and more,
Had boldly stood on that very floor,
And moved with his eloquence, wisdom, and wit,
The heart of each imp of the Bottomless Pit;
And, besides, had old Lucifer's mind so impressed,
That he set him on high above the rest;
Had adopted his plans to knock Liberty over,
And damage her so that she couldn't recover.
The chronicles tell us, in sentence brief,
That Diabolus made him commander-in-chief
Of his forces in Dixie and all the word over;
That he swore a big oath that he'd bring to grief
The noisy humanitarian crew
That had given them all so much to do.
And now he is there to tell them how
Untiringly faithful he's been to that vow;
And how wisely and bravely he's wrought out his
     scheme,
And wakened expectant man from his dream
Of the "good time coming," and made him bow
His head in the dust of despondency low.

He rose, and, his eloquence to inspire,
He first took a drink of liquid fire ;
And then commenced a "masterly speech,"
· The details of which we cannot now reach ;
The most salient points, however, I'll touch ;
And the matter of these will be as much
As will be prudent for me to mention,
For I would not overtax your attention.
    He began with the plainest matter of fact,
All tending to show his consummate tact ;
And to force upon his hearers' convictions
His skill in fulfilling his own predictions,
Made so many years back in the hearing of all
Assembled then in that council-hall.
He told how he set himself first to corrupt
The pulpit and press, the bar and the forum,
Throughout the dominions of "Uncle Sam ;"
And successfully managed his sophisms to cram
In the heads of the leaders of public opinion ;
And 'twas the absurdest and vilest jorum
That ever could possibly hold dominion
In the minds of men who claim to be sane.
Heresy, civil and sacred, he emptied
Into ear, heart, and conscience, a deadly bane ;
Now he coaxed, now bullied, now threatened, now
      tempted,
Leaving no stone unturned his point to gain.

" Behold my success !" said he, with a grin
 That showed all his teeth, " it takes me to win !
 I have gotten a race of political tricksters,
 Such as never before the world has seen ;
 Richelieu, Macchiavelli, and Talleyrand, too,
 Were but fools, when compared with this villainous
   crew.
 And, best of all, they are permanent fixtures
 In the spacious dwelling of ' Uncle Sam ;'
 Hoodwinking for ever with impudent flam
 That simple old soul, till ruin shall run
 Like fiery lava o'er all his domains,
 And the freedom he boasts prove nothing but
   chains.
 Ah! ha! that's a sample of what I've done !"
  Then he went on to show how he got them
   a-fighting
 In the halls of Congress for plunder and wrong ;
 How their power increased and their hands grew
   strong ;
 How they went abroad through the land, de-
   lighting
 The gaping throng with their legerdemain ;
 So perverting each simpleton's moral sight,
 That black appeared white and darkness light,
 Iniquity good, and righteousness vain ;
 Driving mercy before them wherever they went ;

On Slavery's power and extension intent,
And ever on Lucifer's interests bent.
Lucifer, Slavery, Selfishness, Plunder,
Must succeed, all alike, or together go under;
This was their creed, and they stuck to it well;
How well, none so well as this imp could tell.
    Then he told them how journalists, greedy for
      pelf,
Had body and soul sold out to himself,
And had joined with great gusto the rascally herd,
And alike took their cue when he gave them the
      word;
" Though," said he, " it is true, there still are a few
  Who can't be bought over to take such a view
  Of a patriot's duty as I would present it;
  And continue up to this day to resent it.
  But my friends have pretty much put them down,
  And they're rather under the popular frown;
  Still, though hope for their cause from them long
      must have fled,
  I cannot help wishing they all were dead.
  I'd give one of my horns if they'd knock on the
      head
  One *Horace Greeley*, the chief of the band;
  He's the one I have dreaded the most in the land.
  But why talk I thus? Hence, forebodings! away!
  Why intrude on the joy that crowns us to-day?

The victory's ours; there can be no mistake;
Why, we're celebrating dead Freedom's wake!"
('Twas strange, while this imp's sun of joy shone
     so bright,
This cloud should pass o'er it and dim its light!)
In calmer mood, he went on to say
That he couldn't have hoped to gain the day,
With the help of e'en press and politicians;
He must others secure, whose commanding posi-
     tions
Gave them over the people a powerful sway.
"So," said he, "I labored with all my might,
To get the *divines* of the country all right.
Some I found ready—they fell into line;
But others, I knew I couldn't make mine,
Without employing my cunning finesse;
And, perhaps, laying on them a little stress
Of worldly.pressure—so tighten the screws,
That they'd feel it their interest not to refuse
To sail with the popular current along,
That now had set in my favor strong.
I couldn't, of course, hope to get them all;
Yet expected to make a pretty good haul.
And I did; why, would you believe it, my fiends?
I succeeded beyond my most sanguine hopes;
They flocked to my standard in perfect troops,
And helped with a will to accomplish my ends.

. The way I managed was simply thus :
I set my new allies at work hard and fast ;
And they soon stirred up a tremendous muss,
By denouncing the crime of ' political preaching,'
And raging against ' abolitionist teaching ;'
And multitudes took up the matter at last ;
Swore they'd stop the parsons' bread and butter,
If they dared another word to utter,
That bore on political questions at all !
Church-members by thousands took part in the
  movement,
And vowed there must be a decided improvement
In the way that their pastors handled their text,
Or they'd better look out, for they'd get themselves
  vexed.
' Give us Gospel !' they clamored, 'that's what we
  want,
And none of your anti-slavery rant !'
So, fearing the vengeance that threatened to fall,
Lots of them hastened to stand from under
The terrible bolts of this popular thunder.
Some only consented to *hold their peace*,
Hoping thus to escape some conscience-twinges ;
But others swung round like doors on their hinges ;
I'm mostly indebted of course to these,
Though I thank the others for easing my task,
By wearing the *non-committal* mask.

My work was now easy, I felt assured,
With this competent help I'd thus secured.
Some day we will give them a *warm* reception,
To show how we valued their useful deception !"
A cheer from the crowd this sally met;
Such a cheer ! if you'd heard it you'd never forget.

    He went on to say, when the cheering was over,
That it didn't take long, then, the land to cover
With *conservative* pulpits and *pious* presses
Which attributed all the benignant graces
To the hatefulest monster begotten by devils,
The fruitfulest conglomeration of evils
That ever grew 'midst the human race,
Its indelible shame, its eternal disgrace.
He called it his " beautiful Pandora's box,"
And " the splendid American Paradox ;"
And tears of joy down his face did fall,
As he told how zealous those parsons were all.
" Why," said he, " these saints talk like this to their
        people,"
(Here he whined, and mimicked a pious face :)
" ' My brethren, there doesn't stand a church steeple
Beneath which a greater heresy's taught,
Nor a doctrine with greater mischief fraught,
Than that which asserts that all men are made free ;
A mere glittering generality
Is that dogma of Human Equality.

Cursed be Canaan, the patriarch said,
A servant of servants for aye shall he be ;
That settles the negro's status, you see !
Would ye take, then, the thought in your foolish
　　head,
That opposes high Heaven's most plain decree ?
I beseech you, let the negro be !
He's far better off in his present station ;
And it is at the risk of your soul's damnation,
If you dare to commit the impious folly,
Of laying rude hands on such property holy.
Besides, if you touch that divine Institution,
You're committing a breach of the Constitution !
Run on for a while at that radical rate, 　　[State,
And you'll pull to the ground the whole fabric of
For the base that it stands on is Slavery,
And Slavery stands on the Bible, you see !'
Thus the hypocrites talk," the fiend said.
" No wonder our cause has successfully sped !
With Press, Politician, and Parson to back,
The ' chivalrous ' sons of Dixie may crack
Their whips on the naked hide of the black,
Either woman or man, and none dare ask: ' Why
Do you practise this devilish cruelty ?'
　　But more of the Press, or rather that portion
That has shown to our cause or respect or devo-
　　tion ;—

Why, some of the piousest journals plead
With all their might for Slavery's creed;
While more than one Christian book-printing So-
    ciety
Have long ago felt the plain propriety
Of expunging from all their pages each plea
That may squint at the guilt of slavery.
The very school-books are expurgated
Of every sentence that may be rated
As giving the merest hint that may seem
To favor Freedom, that tabooed theme.
Brother-devils, oh! isn't this most glorious?—
This American ' Index Expurgatorius !' "
    The orator then presented to view,
How the cause of Slavery flourished and grew;
How, when Press and Pulpit were muzzled and
    quiet,
Or else had sold out to the " soul-driving " crew,
The knights of the lash did exult and riot;
And mean politicians bowed at their feet,   [do,
And besought them to say what more they should
In order their lordly wishes to meet,
And give them full proof of their servile devo-
    tion;
And how, that, the ball being well set in motion,
One slice, then another, of fair territory
Was purchased, or conquered, and eagerly thrown

In the ravenous jaws of Lucifer's pet;
How, the more it had, the more it would get—
Twas a long but a very delightful story;
And the fiend waxed warm with the pleasing re-
    cital
Of how his pains-taking had met its requital;
How Fugitive Slave Laws were made and enforced;
How the hounds of the South o'er the free North
    coursed,
And the runaway seized in their bloody jaws,
And, *sumptibus publicis*,* dragged him along
To his horrible doom, the coffle and thong;
While crafty statesmen the populace held,
And, their generous instincts rebelling, quelled
By crying: " Friends, let's obey the laws!
Let's stand by the Union and Constitution,
Which sustain this '*peculiar* institution!'"

    " But," said he, " to persuade them there were
    not decrees
And laws that were higher than any of these,
Was too much for a *statesman's* abilities;
But when *divine doctors* said that wasn't so,
What could they do, but their scruples forego?
The more so, when, as I've already reported,
They preached that the Bible this system sup-
    ported.

                 * At the public expense.

There were other popular whims, moreover,
From which I once thought' they would never re-
      cover;
Thus, 'twas tough to induce them to throw away
Their characteristic love of fair play:
Some would clamor for this when a victim they
      saw
Sent back to his fetters by one-sided law:
And they cursed such law; and they questioned
      the grace   [race;
Of the whole man-stealing and slave-catching
And gave them and their churches all to the devil,
An act, some would say, more honest than civil!
But again some sound doctor, with might and
      main,
Would argue the matter as thus: 'My men,   ›
I assure you you're not at all orthodox;
And you're lacking in Christian charity,
Or such hard and merciless verbal knocks
You would spare our brethren, the 'Chivalry.'
Their cause you traduce is a righteous cause;
These laws you decry are beneficent laws;
And you'll find it so, if you'll be so good
As to study well the Levitical Code.
I refer you to *Thornwell, Palmer, Van Dyke*,
And as many such saints North and South as you
      like,

Who'll give you a *proper* interpretation
Of all the Mosaic Slave Legislation.
Trust *them*, I beseech you, and sternly reject
The '*isms*' of every radical sect :   [*Beechers*,
Cut loose from the *Tyngs, Cheevers, Thompsons*, and
They're a pestilent set of heretical teachers:
And mark! ne'er hear *Phillips* or *Garrison* more,
For they'll hurry your soul to the devil, sure.
Take Southerners for your political teachers,
And *South-side saints* for your only preachers.
Now, why should you frown on that Christian
          slaveholder ?
You certainly must be more reckless, and bolder
Blasphemers than I ever took you to be,
If you say that his piety stands for naught,
Because he his lawful chattel has caught!
Let me tell you, in Church Communion
He ranks as a regular 'A No. 1!'
Why scowl on that honest mechanic?   He
Did quite right in forging the chain for that black,
Who ungratefully turned on his master his back.
Why glower on that merchant for selling a whip
Wherewith to scourge that base runaway sore,
And teach him to wrong his owner no more ?
That mechanic and merchant are both *devout* men !
You should pause before you find fault with them,
          when

The wine of communion they solemnly sip,
And eat of the sacramental bread,
And to all the vain things of the world seem
    dead—
And when Bibles and Tracts they dispense in pro-
    fusion.   [sion,
What! say that those men are with sin in collu-
Or are ever the victims of guilty delusion?
Delusion! When such is the strength of their
    piety,
They're the patrons of every worthy society;
And their names are repeatedly seen in print
Appended to figures that show no stint!
O shame! never harbor hard thoughts again
Concerning such generous Christian men!

    And then, don't you know the Apostle Paul
Sent Onesimus back to his lawful thrall?
Can you wish a more striking proof than this,
That there is nothing in slavery at all amiss?
Let a runaway slave just stop at *my* door,
And I tell you, sirs, as sure as fate,
I'd deliver him up to his master straight.
Yes, sirs, I would; and I'd even do more;
I'd send back my dearest friend—my mother,
As readily as I would another!
What a trifle were this little self-abnegation,
When yielded to just and wise legislation!

Away with your infidel nonsense!—pshaw!
Don't talk to me of a " Higher Law." ' "
  Thus the fiend quoted a learned D.D.,
And seemed to enjoy it with unctuous glee;
And said he, " We'll some day have a rousing fire,
And promote our good friend to the rank of a *fryer*,
For the zeal with which he's upheld the laws,
And pleaded so well our noble cause."
  He then proceeded, in voluble phrase,
To show his success in a thousand ways,   [hand
When conscience-seared wretches joined hand in
To give him unlimited sway in the land :
And among the rest of the things, said he,
" The doom of Freedom's a settled thing,
  Since the world will have it that ' Cotton is King,'
And with clamorous voice cry, ' So let it be!'
Ah! the slave to his chariot-wheels is bound fast,
And will stay there so long as his kingdom shall
        last;
And never you fear that its downfall is near,
While the mammonist feeds and gets fat on its
        cheer.
If an imp like me may candid be—
And I think I may in such company—
I say, Out on the mean hypocritical trick
Of quoting the Bible for Slavery!
'Tis enough to make a devil sick!

You know the secret of Slavery's hold—
It fills up the coffers of men with gold:
That's the reason God's image is bought and sold;
And the monster, by sermon and resolution,
Is so often declared a 'divine institution!'
(How the numbers have waned who called slave-
      holding 'sin,'
Since that genius invented the Cotton-Gin,
Which rolls up the profits a hundred-fold!)
That's why 'it is wrong that the slave should be
      freed,'
And 'it's dreadful to teach little niggers to read,'
Why, woman's flesh with the whip one may blister,
And with cowhide and toil worry out a man's life;
That's why it is lawful to part man and wife,
Tear parent from child, and brother from sister;
And offer for sale on the auction-block
A man's superabundance of human stock;.
Among which, not seldom, may happen to be
The fruit of his lust—his own progeny!
By the by, there's a phase coinciding with this,
Which is too rich an item for me to miss."
(He said this with a leer.) "It's quite right, you
      see,
That *Beauty* may help a man's fortune to make,
When exchanged for the cash of the lecherous
      rake!

All this, in a lump, and in fine, is the reason
They brand abolitionist doctrine as treason;
And preach that Slavery's God's own plan
To convert the benighted African!
    But still, though I'd cast so much poison and
        death
In each moral well and political fount,
That Justice began to labor for breath,
And Freedom looked pallid, and wasted away;
I didn't forget to take into account,
That a sudden reäction might come some day,
For, as I have said, I couldn't strike dead
The honest convictions of all the divines;
Nor their fullest expression in speech could I stay;
And a smart little number were left, whom they led
To bend at a purer Religion's shrines,
And to pray that Freedom's sceptre may wave,
Till its blessings should come to every slave.
And some editors, too, and some statesmen were
      left,
Whom my cunning cantraps had never bereft
Of the hope that the nation may yet be delivered;
And this ugly and barbarous structure of crime
By the lightning of Heaven to fragments be shiv-
      ered;
And the temple of Freedom yet stand sublime,
Overarching the world through coming time.

Ah! ha! but I'd well taken care of all that,
And fixed up a plan to defeat it flat.
Down in Dixie I'd filled up their heads with a no-
    tion
That I knew would some day stir up a commotion,
And, if needed, settle the business, pat!
To speak in metaphorical strain,
(A style of which, may be, I'm rather too vain,)
Thirty years ago a brat I'd begotten
In a South-Carolinian's fertile brain,
A fitting companion and friend for King Cotton;
And, when grown to maturity, worthy to reign
Co-sovereign with him o'er that bamboozled na-
    tion: .
Up yonder they christened it ' Nullification.'
Dixie gladly adopted this ugly abortion,
Yet handled the thing with commendable caution;
For they hardly knew what to do with it at first,
And its nearest relation got nearly the worst
Of the bargain, for making too much of my pet;
So that he was constrained, willy-nilly, to let
The monster awhile in concealment be hid,
Till the land was of certain antipathies rid.
He hoped that the time was not very distant,
When he could make it appear consistent
For ' Chivalry's' every valiant son
To make its avowal a *sine qua non.*

That day has come! *full-grown* they display
This hideous thing to the light of day.
It's so, my dear imps ; true, they've changed the
    name ;
But the creature is every whit the same."
  But hold! I cannot run on at this rate ;
Or I'll tire your patience, as sure as fate.
This imp was so wordy, his language so florid,
And he talked so long, that the thought is horrid,
Of inflicting upon you the rest of his speech,
For into the " wee sma' hours " it would reach.
He embraced, in the course of his dissertation,
All the stunning events that have passed in this
    nation ;
He dwelt upon presidential campaigns ;
Fillibustering, too, in each ramification ;
He spoke of Jimmy Buchanan's election,
And what followed, as proving the utter rejection
Of all that would promise the regeneration
From Slavery's curse of this blinded nation ;
Of the freemen's blood, that, on Kansas' plains,
Was first poured out to arrest the tide
Of tyranny, sweeping the nation wide ;
And how, in spite of those martyrs' gore,
His policy triumphed yet the more.
He gloated over the " Dred Scott Decision,"
As helping along the country's division—

Division, of course, preliminary,
As was plainly shown by this devil wary,
To a Slavery-worshipping Reconstruction,
That could but end in the final destruction
Of the nation not only, but Freedom, moreover,
Through the tribes of mankind the wide world
    over.
   He told of party corruption and strife,
That was worrying out the nation's life ;
And said that three fourths of the people were will-
    ing
That oppression's blood-stained rod should rule
A country once trained in Liberty's school,
And seemed to have had there the best of drilling.
   He chuckled delightedly whilst he told,
How truculent partisans greedily sold
The nation's honor for office and gold ;
How they cheated by regular system and rule ;
How the " Old Public Func." was his pliant tool ;
Readily taking his gentlest hint,
And truckling to traitors without any stint ;
How he took for advisers a graceless batch
Of secesh fire-eaters, ready to catch
At every chance to seize on the spoils
Of office, and cunningly wind the toils
Round the helpless limbs of poor " Uncle Sam ;"
And by dint of the logic of Hell to cram

The doctrine of "State Rights" down the throats
Of the gullible masses ; and so, by their votes,
Secure the triumph of Slavery's cause,
And strengthen its arm by more stringent laws ;
How he had secured the Sons of the Brogue
On the side of Oppression ; and every rogue
With the " gift of the gab," 'and employed their
      glib tongues
In declaiming on Dixie's "grievous wrongs ;"
How he'd fleeced " Uncle Sam " of gun, powder,
      and shell,
And got Dixie ready to pitch in pell-mell,
And blow the old Union up with a crash,
That would all its free institutions smash.
And then he told how, when all was ready,
With gaze unintermitting and steady,
They watched for a pretext to strike the blow
That should lay the form of Liberty low ;
And how, to give them the best of a start, he
Had split up the Democratic Party ;
Making way to set in executive throne
A man who, in every nerve and bone,
To Freedom's tottering cause was devoted ;
And how by that stroke was the pretext supplied
To knock Freedom over, the Union divide,
And the triumph of·Might over Right decide.

"Oh! ho!" said this devil, "how my eyes
    gloated,
To see how nicely I'd opened the way
For setting a-going a bloody fray,
That should end in the wildest devastation
That ever swept o'er a devoted nation!"
    And now he had come to the pith of his story;
For nothing tickles a devil so much,
As to witness, or even remember such
Wild scenes of strife and battle gory,
Such savage collision, and martial rage,
As have lately filled our historic page.
He dilated on what he called the "fun"
Of the first shot fired from rebel gun;
And rushed on with language faster and faster,
In describing each crushing Union disaster;
How hosts of the Union heroes fell,
In fighting Secession, Slavery, and Hell;
How the barbarous traitors denied to those braves,
'Neath the slave-cursed sod, their well-earned
    graves;   •
How of patriots' bones were made trinkets rare,
To set off the charms of the Rebel fair;
How imprisoned martyrs languished and died
By thousands, in Richmond's loathsome dens,
And remoter Southern prison-pens,
By slow starvation savagely plied;

And how Northern households mourning went
For their sons to such hopeless slaughter sent:
And you ought to have heard this devil crack
Of the generalship of "Little Mac!"
    He laughed at the popular indignation
Which first met this Rebel manifestation;
And how quickly that stream he was able to dam,
By the help of his friends, Vallandigham,
Cox, Brooks, Burr, Ben and Fernando Wood,
And a hundred others just as good,
With plenty besides of the smaller fry,
Who could lustily yell the party cry.
    Then he told how the Rebels ravaged the seas,
And on every water succeeded with ease
In sweeping the Yankee commerce away;
How the Rebel flag was floating gay
From many a steamship's and gunboat's mast!
And, to show how sure it was, at last,
That the Union was gone, he told how, abroad,
The Aristocrats did the Rebels applaud,
And help them, moreover, with ships, and loans,
And martial equipments, and ammunition,
Feeling sure of Treason's full fruition,
And that soon they would hear "Uncle Sam's"
    death-groans.
    He dwelt with delight on the devils' work
Which his faithful servants had done in New-
    York;

And told his delighted hearers the tale
• That has made Humanity's cheek turn pale—
Though, of what the *applause* of *traitors* earned—
Of how harmless men were hanged and burned,
On account of their owning a dusky skin—
Atrocious, unpardonable sin !—
How shillalies descended with murderous whacks
On the heads of the poor, defenceless blacks ;
How dark-skinned orphans were burnt out of
  home,
And, shelterless, forced abroad to roam ;
And how Seymour the Syndic condescends
To call those assassins his " very dear friends !"
"Ha ! ha !" said the imp, "what matter to us,
The few lovers of Liberty making a fuss
In praise of Abe Lincoln's Proclamation,
Decreeing the slaves' emancipation ?
We may laugh to scorn such impotent acts
While opposed to them stand these *telling facts.*"
  Thus this imp, with eye like electric fire,
Soared onward in eloquence higher and higher,
Till he carried his hearers again away ;
And Old Nick once more succumbed to the sway
Of his brilliant bursts of rhetorical thunder ;
And surely there never was thunder profound-
  er !
The patron *saint* he well might be

Of the demagogues of the " Chivalry,"
Or the dough-faced spouters for Slavery.
   He paused in his speech ; and, though he'd not
      done,
His audience rose to their feet, every one ;
You ne'er saw so enthusiastic a crew.
The old Chief rose, too, and he gave them the
      cue ;
In tones that a mortal ear would stun,
' Three cheers !" cried he, " for Slavery !
Three more for *my sort* of Democracy !
Pet name for most mean Aristocracy ;
Its real import, *Dulocracy !*
Go it, my devils ! thunder it out !
Let the world up yonder hear your shout !
That's glorious, my devils ! well done, well done !
And now three more for Jeff Davis & Co. !
That's good—that's capital !   There—so, so !
Don't split yourselves, devils, there's one more to
      go ;
Three *special* good ones for Seymour and ' friends !'
They've aided our cause beyond all praise ;
Their devotion to us all other transcends ;
Shout, then, till your voices the roof shall raise !"
They shouted ; 'tis well you heard not that shout,
The lamp of your life would have been blown
      out !

They shouted; and true as Diabolus spoke,
The lofty roof of that dome was broke,
And was all blown away; and where it fell
It would puzzle the shrewdest devil to tell.
And mortals just then were heard to talk
About having felt an earthquake shock!

But look! What strange vision is that over-
    head,   [dread
Where the dome so late spanned, that with sudden
Convulses the features of every devil?
What sad foreboding behold they of evil?
    Ah! there stands a radiant form aloft
With a visage that beams with triumph and scorn;
And high in her fair right hand is borne
A banner resplendent with glittering stars,
And legends covering it over, that scoffed
At Secession, and Hell, and every plan
They'd devised to accomplish the ruin of man.
Thereon were inscribed, in letters of light,
Victories won by the stout arm of Right;
And victories, also, that should be yet won,
And pledged by the deeds already done:
For a Heaven-commissioned sceress was she
Who waved that Flag of Liberty.
There were other triumphs, besides, on record,
Won, or *to be* won, not by the sword,

But by the unbloody and wise legislation
Of a chastened, mourning, repentant nation;
Victories o'er passions and feelings unkind;
Triumphs o'er prejudice mad and blind;
Retrieving the wrongs that, for hundreds of years,
Had covered the land with blood and tears;
Lifting a down-trodden, outraged race
To its long-denied yet God-given place,
Where the chances of life and its joys are as fair
As Humanity's children's anywhere.

The eyes of that rabble, with hopeless gaze,
Were fixed on those legends, and stars' bright rays
That studded that glorious flag of the free,
The fair symbol of coming jubilee,
No more to be trod in the mire of disgrace.
And as they gazed, tormented, amazed,
On the Hell-scathing emblems that banner re-
    vealed
On every fold of its dazzling field,
Those devices were suddenly all erased;
And pictures of glory, that withered their sight,
Were revealed to their view in heaven's own
    light.

There were myriads of freemen marching along,
With victorious tramp, and exultant song;
And millions of bondmen, now set free,
Had joined in that march of victory;

Before them the herds of Rebellion fled,
Each seeking in vain to hide his head
From the vengeful flash of those freemen's brands,
Held firm in the grasp of unflinching hands.
    The scene then changed; and the next view ranged
Through all the cities and towns of the nation
These fiends had doomed to extermination:
They beheld vast crowds of men, now free
From the bonds of party tyranny,
Casting their ballots with resolute will—
Ballots headed, "UNION AND LIBERTY!"
O Diabolus! that was a bitter pill!
And down thy throat it had to go,
Sadly against thy stomach, I trow!
    But, presto! The election scene is gone;
And another, as blasting to Satan, is shown.
All at once there are thousands of pulpits revealed,
And every pulpit with preacher is filled;
And before them sit crowds with attentive ears;
And the words of those preachers each devil hears:
For by powers mysterious those spirits possessed,
The visions both eye and *ear* addressed.
    The preachers were all denouncing Secession;
Not only Secession, but *Slavery* as well—
The hateful cause of rebellious aggression;

Denouncing them both as begotten in Hell,
And fit only together with devils to dwell.
They prayed to the God of Hosts to fight
With his conquering arm, for Freedom and Right.
And among the divines that preached thus and
    prayed,
Were most of the men who had lent their aid,
Either active or passive, in former days,
To Lucifer's plan, Freedom's fane to raze!
As true as you live, once pro-slavery preachers
Were now what he cursed, and called "freedom-
    screechers;
He was mad when he called them that ugly name;
But who the poor checkmated devil could blame?
    That vision, too, passed from the field of sight;
And a number of others as galling quite,
Moved in rapid order before their view,
Until dizzy and faint each devil grew;
And when the last picture had faded in air,
And evanished, also, that angel fair,
There was heard from invisible choirs to rise
A chorus of sweet, thrilling harmonies,
Filling those fiends with dreadful surprise—
For music a devil with agony hears,
Especially such as now smote their ears.
List to the anthem!—ay, let it be sung,
Not only by angel but mortal tongue.

Swell the triumph! Raise the song!
Earth and Heaven the notes prolong!
Blessings Heaven sends down to man;
Peace succeeds War's cruel ban.
Broke the proud oppressor's rod
By the strong right hand of God;
Weak the strength of Freedom's foes,
When to vengeance he arose.

Hail, Columbia Now arise!
God accepts thy sacrifice:
Purified from Slavery's stain,
Union now is thine again.
Faithful to thy holy trust,
Lift the prostrate from the dust;
So thy radiance far shall glow,
Brighter for thy days of woe.

Henceforth float, O banner free!
Over land and over sea;
Bear thou to the tribes of earth
Freedom's boon of priceless worth.
Despot's terror, bondman's light,
Chase from earth tyrannic night:
Fling thy gleaming stars on high,
Long to shine in Freedom's sky.

Let the high, inspiring strain
Thrill the air from main to main;
Might and Right join hand in hand;
Mercy's arms enfold the land.
Swell the triumph!   Raise the song!
Earth and Heaven the notes prolong!
Blessings Heaven sends down to thee,
Nation ransomed, saved, and free!

Thus ended the devils' grand jubilee;
Thus was turned to howling their boisterous glee:
The hellish rabble now felt pretty sure
That their frolic was rather premature!
Aghast, they rushed from their council-hall,
Diabolus, eloquent devil, and all;
They sought in the fiery lake to hide
Their deep disappointment and wounded pride,
And confessed, as they plunged in the burning
        flood,
Their weakness in coping with Freedom's God!

POSTSCRIPT.

TIME—APRIL 9, 1865.

So closes my narrative, done up in verse;
It might have been *shorter* and ended *worse;*
And have suited so well the devil's views,
That the lightning would never have brought us
     the news
That makes all the people now feel so jolly;
And that doubtless convinces the "Rebs" of their
     folly,
In humoring Lucifer up to his bent,
By trying to smash up this Government.
   When Jeff and Lee out of Richmond did clear,
Each with a very large "flea in his ear;"
And later, when Grant, with strategic bag,
Snared those hosts of "Johnnies," "bobtail, tag,
     and rag,"
It seemed as though most of the vision bright
Which brought on those devils' frolic a blight,
Had turned out a matter of history, quite!

Do the poet the justice, then, to suppose
That he saw some distance beyond his nose.
But a fig for the poet!   Give to the men,
Who have struggled so long in the serpent's den,
The justice, the honor, the praise that is meet;
The reptile of treason lies dead at their feet;
Their well-wielded weapons have slavery killed;
Their victories the nation with joy have thrilled.
Hurrah for our soldiers! the noble, the brave,
Whose heaven-nerved arms did our country save!
Hurrah for the chieftains who've led them on!
Grant, Sherman, Kilpatrick, and Sheridan;
Ben Butler as well—for his record proud,
Shall never be dimmed by obloquy's cloud!
Hurrah for all who for Country and Right
Have headed our heroes with valor and might!
Hurrah for the soldiers with *sable faces!*
Who have helped put the rebels through their
        paces;
And who made " dare ole massas' " coat-tails fly,
As they scampered from Richmond with speed so
        high!
Hurrah for the States of the Union grand,
That now on the rock of Liberty stand!
Hurrah for the statesmen, who firm have stood
'Gainst both bribe and threat of the traitor brood!

For " Father Abraham," honest and true;
The man who has given " the devil his due;"
And who, in this hour of our nation's glory,
Is reminded, no doubt, " of a little story!"
   Hurrah for the wives, sweethearts, sisters, and
      mothers,
Who have given their sons, lovers, husbands, and
      brothers
For their country's salvation ; and stifled the cries
That sought vent from the heart's deep agonies!
   A sorrowful sigh and a silent tear
For the thousands henceforth to their country
      dear;
Who have fallen while grappling with Treason's
      horde,
And whose forms lie so still 'neath the cold green-
      sward.
   But to God be high praise for the victory
That *indeed* makes Columbia the " Land of the
      Free !"

ANOTHER POSTSCRIPT!

——•••——

ABRAHAM LINCOLN,

DIED

A MARTYR FOR COUNTRY AND FREEDOM,

APRIL 15, 1865.

Mournfully falls the measured toll
Of the funeral bell on the nation's soul;
And the fretted dome of cathedral grand,
And the roof of the humblest fane in the land,
Alike resound with the requiem's wail;
And the preacher's voice, as he dwells on the tale
That has changed to mourning the joy of the land;
How the ruler, faithful and pure, by the hand
Of the vile assassin and traitor, died
In the hour of the country's triumph and pride.

What! has Lucifer taken fresh heart, and deemed
His cause from defeat may yet be redeemed;
Not he! there he lies in the gulf below,
Where our narrative left him short time ago:
And no resurrection his hopes shall know.

   'Tis the last spent ripple of Treason's wave,
Whose impulse at first the devil gave;
'Tis Tophet's senior scholars' act;
'Tis a blow, though stunning, that more impact
Has the friends of freedom and Union drawn;
That hastens, not hinders, the rosy dawn,
Presaging the rise of Liberty's sun,
To set no more till Time's work is done.

   Yes, mourn, sad people! let every bell
Roll forth the *good man's* funeral knell!
Then, O nation! arise from thy prostrate woe,
To strike at Treason thy final blow!
And, the days of thy fiery trial past,
Thy sins atoned and forgiven at last,
Thy banner of freedom for ever shall wave
O'er Secession and Slavery's hated grave!

www.ingramcontent.com/pod-product-compliance
Lightning Source LLC
Chambersburg PA
CBHW030011030726
47499CB00008B/2994